Butterfly Count

BY SNEED B. COLLARD III

ILLUSTRATED BY

PAUL KRATTER

Holiday House / New York

In memory of my Great-Grandmother
Nora Bell Smith, a true pioneer
S. B. C.

To my Father
P. K.

Acknowledgments

The author would like to thank Dr. Diane Debinski of Iowa State University
for her extensive assistance in helping him understand the world of butterflies.

The illustrator extends a very special thanks to Erin Bricker and
her mother, Darby. He would also like to give thanks to Mike Gorman
and to Ken Robertson of the Illinois Natural History Survey for his expertise
on the tallgrass prairie.

The publisher would like to thank entomologist Louis Sorkin
of the American Museum of Natural History for his assistance.

Library of Congress Cataloging-in-Publication Data
Collard, Sneed B.
Butterfly count / by Sneed B. Collard; illustrated by Paul Kratter.—1st ed.
p.   cm.
Summary: Amy and her mother look for a very special butterfly while attending
the annual Fourth of July Butterfly Count at a prairie restoration site. Includes factual
information about butterflies and how to attract and watch them.
ISBN 0-8234-1607-0 (hardcover)
[1. Butterflies—Fiction. 2. Butterfly watching—Fiction.
3. Wildlife conservation—Fiction. 4. Prairies—Fiction.]
I. Kratter, Paul, ill. II. Title.
PZ7.C67749 Bu 2002
[E]—dc21   2001024114

THE FOURTH OF JULY.

I wake up to see the picture on the wall.
"*Speyeria idalia,*" I whisper. "The regal fritillary."

My mother put up the picture soon after
I was born. When I was old enough,
she told me the story.

"Amy," my mom said, "that was the animal your great-great-grandmother Nora Belle loved most. When her family brought her west from New York, miles of tallgrass prairie stretched in every direction. Each summer, regal fritillaries by the thousands danced over the bluestem grasses, setting the prairie afire with butterfly wings."

"Before she died," my mother finished, "Nora Belle wanted nothing more than to see those fritillaries dance again."

I never met my great-great-grandmother, but my mom and I still live near where she and her family farmed. Unfortunately, the regal fritillaries are gone. Their prairie homes are farms and houses now.

But today, I think. Today, maybe I will get to see a regal fritillary for the very first time. Because today is the day of the annual Fourth of July Butterfly Count.

Mom drives out of town until we reach a large sign that reads
NORA BELLE PRAIRIE RESTORATION PROJECT. This land used to be my
great-great-grandmother's farm. She gave it to a conservation group
that turned it back into a natural prairie.

When I was still a baby, volunteers began planting prairie plants and
seeds where my great-great-grandparents' crops once grew. Every couple
of years, they mowed and burned the fields to give native prairie plants
a chance to outgrow the weeds that always tried to take over.

Little by little, more prairie animals moved in: meadowlarks, foxes, rabbits, and voles. Best of all, butterflies moved in: swallowtails, sulphurs, coppers, hairstreaks, checkerspots, blues, cloudywings, duskywings, skippers, and several kinds of fritillaries.

But the regal fritillary has never returned. Each Fourth of July, my mom and I look for them. And every year, we are disappointed. But today, I tell myself, maybe it will come back.

Along with the other butterfly counters, I move out across the fields. With my brand-new butterfly guide and checklist, I can pick out a monarch, a black swallowtail, a mourning cloak, and a great spangled fritillary. I also spot a painted lady—I know that one because we raised some in school last year.

Scott, a biology student, helps me with some harder butterflies. "For the blue butterflies and many of the skippers," Scott tells me, "you need to see both sides of the wings to identify exactly which species you're looking at."

By noon, I am hungry. My mom and I spread a checkered cloth and join everyone else for a picnic.

As people munch sandwiches and potato chips, I listen to their stories of the different butterfly species they've found. The butterfly names seem magical: clouded sulphur, eastern tailed-blue, gorgone checkerspot, southern cloudywing, tawny-edged skipper. My mom turns to me and says, "Amy, just think. All across the United States, Canada, and Mexico, people are counting butterflies just like we are."

In the afternoon, I walk with my mom and we count butterflies together. We see some good ones, like a common wood nymph, a variegated fritillary, and a red admiral.

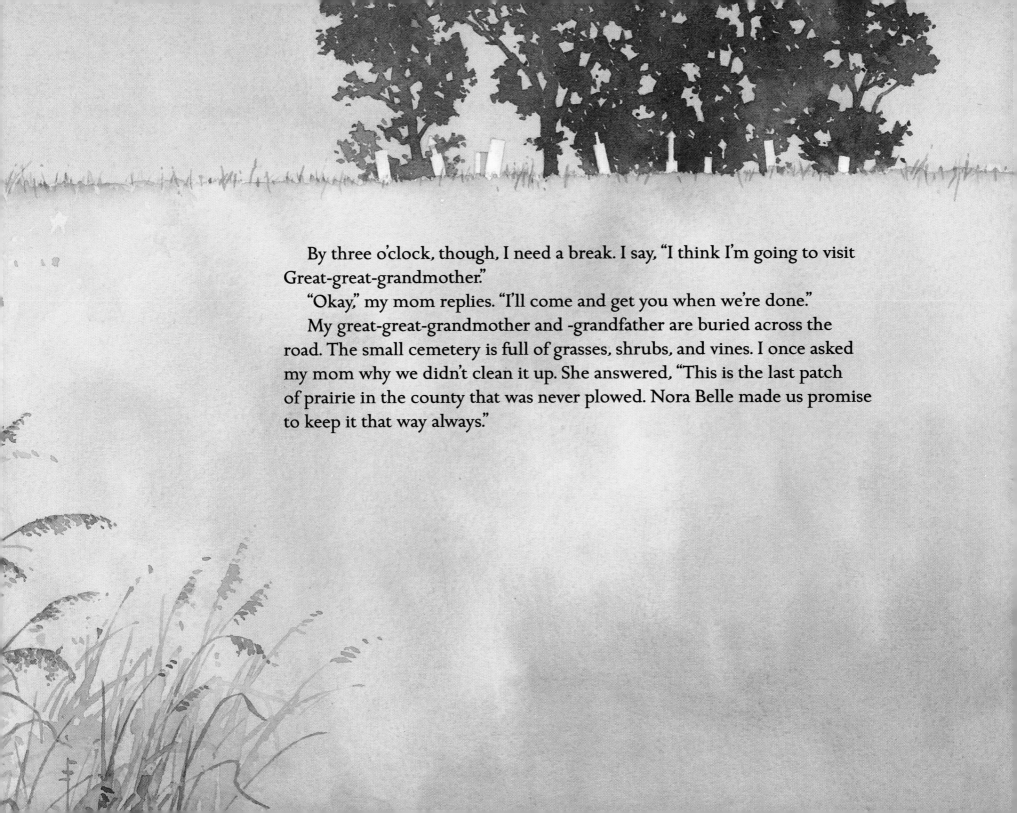

By three o'clock, though, I need a break. I say, "I think I'm going to visit
Great-great-grandmother."

"Okay," my mom replies. "I'll come and get you when we're done."

My great-great-grandmother and -grandfather are buried across the
road. The small cemetery is full of grasses, shrubs, and vines. I once asked
my mom why we didn't clean it up. She answered, "This is the last patch
of prairie in the county that was never plowed. Nora Belle made us promise
to keep it that way always."

A tall elm tree grows next to the gravesites, and I lie down in the shade. Before long, I fall asleep.

When I wake, I hear my mother calling from across the road. I am just about to leave, when I see it.

It sits perched on a purple coneflower, sipping nectar.

At first glance, the butterfly looks a lot like other fritillaries or a monarch. But then I notice the purplish tint and two rows of spots on the butterfly's hind wings.

I step back, almost afraid to breathe. "Mom!" I call. "Mom! Come quick!"

My mom rushes over, looking worried. The butterfly has moved to another bloom, but it is still there. I silently point.

We watch for several moments. Then my mom says, "I should have known. Your great-great-grandmother was keeping the fritillaries safe until . . ."

"Until what?" I ask her.

She looks at me and says, "Until we realized that we missed them."

That night, we eat barbecue and, later, watch fireworks. They make loud booming noises and explode into splashes of purple, red, yellow, blue, white, and orange. To me, they look just like . . . butterflies.

Butterflies in This Book

Although the regal fritillary is endangered in most of its former range, many of the other butterflies in this book continue to thrive. Some can probably be found near your home.

Southern Cloudywing
(Thorybes bathyllus)
The adults of this species live only for a week or two. To attract females, males sit in one spot four or five feet above the ground. Southern cloudywings can be found in almost any open place from the eastern U.S. to the Midwest.

Red Admiral
(Vanessa atalanta)
A common butterfly in parks and yards across the U.S., the red admiral flies quickly and "crazily." It feeds on nectar, but prefers eating tree sap, fermenting fruit, and bird droppings. Yuck!

Black Swallowtail
(Papilio polyxenes)
This large, greenish black beauty feeds on red clover, milkweed, and thistles. It lays its eggs on carrots, celery, and other plants of the parsley family. Look for black swallowtails from southern Canada to northern South America.

Tawny-edged Skipper
(Polities themistocles)
With their "fat" bodies and half-folded wings, many skippers look more like moths than butterflies. The small tawny-edged skipper lives across most of the U.S. and Canada, especially around lawns, vacant lots, pastures, and other grassy areas.

Painted Lady
(Vanessa cardui)
This butterfly lives on every continent except Australia and Antarctica. Every spring, millions migrate north from central Mexico. Look for them almost everywhere!

Eastern Tailed-Blue
(Everes comyntas)
This small, pretty butterfly feeds on clover and other plants in the pea family. In early summer, eastern tailed-blues gather around mud puddles. The tiny "tails" at the back of each hind wing set them apart from other midwestern blue butterflies.

Great Spangled Fritillary
(Speyeria cybele)
Smaller and paler than the regal fritillary, the great spangled is the most common fritillary in eastern North America. It lives in a wide variety of open habitats in southern Canada and the northern half of the U.S.

Gorgone Checkerspot

(Chlosyne gorgone)
Found mostly in the midwest and western U.S. and Canada, this smaller butterfly can be found in many habitats, from open woodlands, to stream-sides, to prairies. Adults feed on nectar from yellow flowers. Caterpillars feed on leaves of plants in the sunflower family.

Variegated Fritillary

(Euptoieta claudia)
The variegated fritillary—unlike other fritillaries—has no silver spots on its underwings. It is also smaller and *much* more common than its rarer relative. Variegated fritillaries can be found from southern Canada all the way to Argentina. Look for them in open, sunny places.

Monarch

(Danaus plexippus)
One of the world's most famous—and largest—butterflies, the monarch migrates. Like the regal fritillary, monarchs sport bold black and orange colors that warn birds of their bad taste.

Mourning Cloak

(Nymphalis antiopa)
The large mourning cloak is often one of the first butterflies to come out in spring. It can live up to eleven months, making it one of our "oldest" butterflies. It is found throughout most of North America, so keep an eye out!

Common Wood Nymph

(Cercyonis pegala)
This butterfly can be found in most regions of the U.S. and Canada. Known for large "eye-spots" on its underwings, the adult feeds on flower nectar and rotting fruit. It lays its eggs on purpletop and other grasses. The caterpillars hatch in fall, but hibernate for the winter before they begin to feed.

Clouded Sulphur

(Colias philodice)
This common yellow butterfly lives in almost all of the U.S. and Canada. It is especially fond of plants in the pea family, including alfalfa and clover. Look for clouded sulphurs on your lawn.

The Regal Fritillary

(Speyeria idalia)
was once widespread from the eastern U.S. and Canada west to Montana, Colorado, and Oklahoma. One of North America's largest butterflies, it inhabits open marshlands and tallgrass prairies. Adults feed on thistle, pale purple coneflower, butterfly weed, and milkweed. The caterpillars feed almost exclusively on plants in the violet family.

Because of prairie and wetland destruction and the use of pesticides, however, the regal fritillary has disappeared from most of its former homes. The greatest hope for the survival of the regal fritillary and many other butterfly species lies in protecting and restoring their original habitats and in restricting the use of pesticides and other harmful chemicals.

The Fourth of July Butterfly Count

Each summer, the North American Butterfly Association (NABA) sponsors the annual Fourth of July Butterfly Count. On or near July fourth, thousands of volunteers throughout North America gather to identify and count butterflies. They give their lists and counts to NABA, which tabulates the numbers from all the counts.

In 2000, the twenty-sixth annual NABA Fourth of July Butterfly Count was held. Four hundred and twenty-one butterfly counts were held in 44 states, Canada, and Mexico. Altogether, more than 300,000 butterflies of hundreds of different species were counted. These counts provide important information for people working to protect the regal fritillary and other endangered butterfly species. To learn more about the butterfly count and how to promote butterflies in your area, contact the North American Butterfly Association, 4 Delaware Road, Morristown, NJ 07960, or visit their website at http://www.naba.org/

Watching and Attracting Butterflies

One of the wonderful things about butterflies is that you can find them almost everywhere, from your backyard to city parks to wilderness miles away. Some of the best places to see them are areas that have been "overlooked" by people. These include spots along railroad and power line routes, at old factory sites, and in vacant lots and fields. Often the plants that butterflies and their caterpillars eat grow in these overlooked places. Especially common butterfly plants include milkweeds, clovers, goldenrods, honeysuckles, and (of course!) butterfly bushes.

Important: *Before venturing into any private property,* always *get permission from the landowner. Also,* never *look along a rail line, road, or other dangerous place without an adult accompanying you.*

Also keep in mind that you need proper permits to collect many butterfly species and that you can easily injure a butterfly when catching it. For this reason, learn to enjoy and identify butterflies without touching them. A great book about butterfly watching is *Butterflies Through Binoculars: The East* by Jeffrey Glassberg (Oxford University Press, 1999).

To help butterflies in your area, you might think about planting your own butterfly garden. The North American Butterfly Association has published guides that will help you choose what to plant in each part of the country. To learn how to obtain a guide for your part of the country, write to Butterfly Gardens & Habitats, 909 Birch Street, Baraboo, WI 53913.